TWICE
TOLD
TALES

Twicetold Tales is published by Stone Arch Books
A Capstone Imprint
1710 Roe Crest Drive
North Mankato, Minnesota 56003
www.capstonepub.com

Library of Congress Cataloging-in-Publication Data
Snowe, Olivia.
  The sealed-up house / by Olivia Snowe; iillustrated by
Michelle Lamoreaux.
     p. cm. -- (Twicetold tales)
  Summary: In this modern version of Sleeping Beauty,
Brendan is fascinated by the house on Willow Avenue,
and by the story the mysterious school nurse tells him
of the girl trapped within--but though he manages
to free the Sova family, the enchantment still lingers,
even onto the next generation.
  ISBN 978-1-4342-6019-2 (library binding) -- ISBN
978-1-4342-6281-3 (paper over board)
  1. Sleeping Beauty (Tale)--Juvenile fiction. 2. Fairy
tales. 3. Folklore--Germany. 4. Magic--Juvenile
fiction. [1. Fairy tales. 2. Folklore. 3. Magic--Fiction.] I.
Lamoreaux, Michelle, ill. II. Sleeping Beauty. English.
III. Title.
  PZ8.S41763Se 2013
  398.20943--dc23
                                   2013002781

Designer: Kay Fraser
Vector Images:: Shutterstock

Printed in the United States of America in
Stevens Point, Wisconsin.
032013   007227WZF13

The Sealed-Up House

by Olivia Snowe

illustrated by Michelle Lamoreaux

▼▼ STONE ARCH BOOKS™

You know the story.

You've heard it before.

Everyone has.

Now, read it again.

A new twist. A new gasp.

The story is told again.

TWICETOLD.

~1~

The bus ride is *exactly the same*, thought Brendan Miren. He'd hardly looked up from his book since he sat down, right in the front row behind the driver. It was the best seat if you wanted to be left alone. The bullies and jerks always sat way in the back, just like at home.

Home, Brendan thought. He had to stop doing that. This was his home now: a new

town, a new bus—the same lurid shade of
yellow—and a new school. But with his face
in a book, it was easy to pretend he and his
mother still lived back in Three Rivers with
Dad, instead of here in Oldtown, in a two-
bedroom apartment near the railroad.

When the bus reached the curb in front of
school, Brendan looked up. Just like back at
the old school, he'd be last off the bus: even
though he sat right in front, all the other kids
had rushed to the front the moment the driver
slammed on the brakes.

They pushed and shouted and taunted each
other, their toes just crossing the white safety
line. The door folded open and the kids piled
off.

Brendan was always kind of amazed that no
one fell, no one tumbled down the two steps
to the sidewalk and landed on their head. He
waited till the path was clear and got up.

"It looks like chaos," he muttered to

himself as he climbed from his seat, "but it is a complex and well-ordered system."

"Ain't that the truth," the bus driver said. "Have a good day, Brendan."

"You too, Archie," Brendan said, and he enjoyed the hissing sound of the door closing behind him as he walked across the sidewalk toward the school.

~2~

It was a day. Just a day. There were classes and there was hot lunch. There were two snide comments.

The first came from a boy in Brendan's math class, just as the ending bell rang. "Do you guys smell something?" the boy said. Brendan thought his name was Edward, but it might have been Reginald. "I think the new kid forgot his deodorant." Several other boys laughed.

The second came from a girl in the cafeteria. "Ohmigosh," she said, loud enough for several nearby kids to hear, though she whispered to a friend. "Is he really going to eat that?" Brendan looked at the pile of baked beans next to his hot dog and scooped a spoonful into his mouth. The girl said, "Ew."

But at three o'clock, as Brendan left the school—spontaneously deciding to walk home rather than ride the bus—it all became a vague memory. None of it really bothered him. He had his book.

For as long as he could remember, Brendan walked with a book. He used to wander Three Rivers with a book in front of his face. Somehow, he never crossed a street against the light. He never stepped in front of a moving bus or fell into one of the city's rivers.

He did, however, get lost. Often.

And that's what happened today, his third day in his new town. Brendan walked—deep in his book—up hills and down hills, and through parks and past strip malls. He crossed the tracks and crossed them again. But he couldn't stop. He was so close to the end.

Within minutes, he'd read how the hero would save himself and then save the village and then defeat the evil king of the land beyond the mountain.

He reached the last page at the same moment he reached the top of the highest hill in Oldtown. He leaned against a knobby old elm tree and devoured the last chapter. He was really there—in the story, riding alongside the hero through the Haunting Woods and across the River of Fire, into the land beyond the mountain where the evil king ruled with a closed and iron fist.

After he—with the hero—had faced and defeated the evil king and his legion of troll warriors, Brendan closed the book and looked up. The elm tree he'd chosen sat on the long,

sloping lawn of a huge stone house that was covered from foundation to widow's walk with crawling, thick ivy. It was enshrouded in a cloak of overgrown shrubs and weeds so thick that no one could have gotten in or out of that house.

Brendan slipped his book into his bag and stared up at the house. *Abandoned?* he wondered. *A hermit?* he imagined. *A witch?* he supposed.

The sun was setting, and an early-fall wind blew in from the north. His mom wouldn't worry—Brendan was always so responsible and great at looking after himself—but he hurried home anyway, taken with a chill.

~3~

"I saw the craziest house, Mom," Brendan said at breakfast the next day. Mom hardly looked up from her dish of yogurt, berries, and granola. She'd been so distracted since the move. Brendan didn't blame her.

"It was covered with plants and thorns and stuff," he said. "It was like the earth was trying to reclaim it or something."

"Hm," Mom said, still barely hearing him.

"I think it's probably under a spell," Brendan added.

Mom chuckled and shook her head. Her eyes remained glazed over, though, and faraway.

★ ★ ★

What happened at school that day was entirely out of character for Brendan: he spoke to other students. He approached them. He cleared his throat.

"Um," he said to a group sitting on desks and chairs in the back of the room before first hour. "Do you guys know the big house up on the hill, way at the end of Willow Avenue?"

A boy in a hoodie looked up from the laughter and conversation, his jaw hanging open. "Um," he said, "yeah. Everyone knows that house. It's the biggest house in Oldtown."

"And the most famous," said the girl sitting nearest, a short girl with frizzy black hair.

"Guys, he's new here," said another girl. She flashed Brendan a tight-lipped, pale smile. "That's the Sova House. It's haunted."

The boy in the hoodie guffawed. "What are you, five?" he said. "It's not haunted. A crazy guy lives there. I heard he murdered his whole family and still lives there with their corpses and dresses them up and has meals with them and stuff."

The black-haired girl shivered.

"That's ridiculous," said pale-smiling girl.

The black-haired girl ran her hand over her forearm. "My dad says the owner probably lives in the city," she said. "That's why it's all overgrown like that."

Brendan listened, but he could tell none of them really knew. "Thanks," he said. Then he took his seat for class.

~4~

It was lucky, in a way—if you look back on it—that Brendan ate his lunch on the back lawn. And it was lucky that he sat at the picnic table farthest from the school where he thought no one would bother him.

And it was lucky that it turned out that the picnic table he chose was actually the favorite picnic table of a boy known as Chunk and three of his friends.

It was also lucky that Chunk picked Brendan up by the hem of his pants and tossed him face-first from the picnic table.

It was lucky because Brendan went to the nurse, and there he got his scrapes cleaned up and bandaged.

Plus he met the school nurse.

"You're new around here," the nurse said. "When you're the nurse at this school, you get to know the picked-on kids pretty quickly."

"Is it that obvious?" Brendan said. "How do you know I didn't just fall down?"

She gave him a sideways look. "It was Chunk, wasn't it?" she said.

Brendan's eyes went wide.

"It's easy," the nurse said. "The gravel I picked from your knee—it had some yellow paint in it. The only gravel like that is next to the parking lot, right near Chunk's favorite picnic table."

"Ah," Brendan said. "You know, they should really put information like that in the new-student handbook."

The nurse smiled. "You read it?" she said.

"I read everything," Brendan admitted.

She nodded at him. Then her look flashed, like she'd been inspired.

"Say," she said as she turned away from him and flipped on the tap to wash her hands. "You're new, but have you seen the house up on Willow?"

Brendan could hardly believe it. "Yes!" he said. "I've been asking all the kids about it. The Sova House, they called it. No one knows a thing, though."

"No?" the nurse said as she dried her hands. "They didn't tell you it's haunted? Or that the owner is a crazy murderer?"

"Oh, no," Brendan said. "They said all that. But it's not true."

"No, it's not," the nurse said. "But I can tell you its secret."

"Please," Brendan said, hopping down from the exam table.

The nurse tossed her paper towel into the trash. Then she closed the exam room door. The lights seemed to dim. Brendan leaned back against the table.

"It's sealed up," she said in a quiet, almost prayerful voice. "Just like it looks. The place hasn't been opened in years. It must be ten years by now."

Brendan held his breath.

"But they're still in there," she went on. "They'll never leave. They've been locked in there for years and years, dead to the town—dead to the world."

"How," Brendan said, and he found he was whispering. He cleared his throat. "How do you know?"

"I used to live there," she said. "I worked for them. But I couldn't take it anymore. I fled the house. It wasn't long before the ivy and briar and thorns and vines climbed across the walls and windows and the iron fence. I'm glad I left when I did, or I'd be sealed in there with them now."

"But it's a secret," Brendan guessed.

She nodded. "The gravest of secrets," she said.

"Then why are you telling me?" Brendan asked.

She opened the door, and daylight flooded the exam room. "You remind me of the girl," the nurse said.

"The girl?" Brendan said as he hefted his book bag. "There's a girl in there?"

The nurse smiled.

"Why do I remind you of her?" Brendan said.

She thought a moment, standing in the open doorway. "You both have a magic about you," she said. She looked him up and down, and then settled on the heavy book bag that hung from one of his hands.

"Maybe," she said, "it's the books."

5

After the last bell, Brendan couldn't board his bus for home. He couldn't even go home. He had to go back to the house. Now if only he could remember the route he took to get there.

Brendan stood on the sidewalk in front of the school as the dozen or so big yellow buses revved their engines, puffed gray smoke, and chugged away, bringing kids back home.

When the smoke cleared, Brendan scanned the Oldtown streets. He had no idea which way to go.

"Willow Avenue," he muttered to himself. "Which way is Willow Avenue?"

He could have asked someone, but all the kids and bus drivers were gone, and all the faculty—even the few unlucky souls in charge of getting the kids safely on their buses—were inside the school. They were in their offices, no doubt drinking coffee with each other and yapping about which students were failing history and which students were sinfully ugly and which students would probably never hold a job once they got out of this dump.

"But the nurse," Brendan said to himself, "said there's magic in me. In me and the girl and the house."

He opened his book bag and pulled out a thick paperback—a sci-fi novel, the newest in a series he'd been reading since book one.

"The magic is in the books," he said. Then he started walking—and reading.

And it worked. When Brendan finished chapter five—with the settlers' small ship crash-landing on a planet that, it turned out, looked remarkably like their home planet, even though they'd been in space for five generations—he looked up.

And there it was: the Sova House.

It looked somehow more imposing today, maybe because today Brendan planned to approach it. And to get inside.

He put away his paperback and shouldered his book bag. He strode up to the iron gate. It was twice his height, and tangled with thick vines, covered in wide deep-green leaves and long, serrated thorns.

Brendan took a deep breath and carefully put both hands on an iron upright. He pricked his fingers once, twice, a third time—wincing each time. His fingers bled, but he didn't

pull away. He held fast to the upright, and he pushed.

And the gate groaned, and the vines rattled and swung. But it moved. Slowly, the gate scraped across the paved driveway. It rang out like a siren, bellowing from the hilltop of Willow Avenue. Brendan imagined the people of Oldtown getting up from supper, switching off their TVs and video games, hurrying to the windows to gaze up at the Sova House—to see who dared to swing open the huge iron gates.

When it was open enough, he squeezed himself through, and the vines and thorns seemed to reach for his arms and legs. A tendril pulled at his wrist. A thorn scraped the length of his arm from his wrist to the end of his T-shirt's sleeve. A thin line of blood ran like a creek.

But Brendan pushed on. The path was not clear, even beyond the heavy gate. The vines and tendrils reached across the paved path—

itself cracked and weedy, with tall and gnarly growth reaching and struggling for sunlight in the thickly shaded yard. Brendan hacked and pushed, but the vines seemed to fight back. They wrapped around his ankles and tore at his pants. Thorns tore holes in his clothes. Vines whipped across his face.

Brendan stopped, right there on the driveway, halfway to the front door, and he looked down at himself. His clothes were ripped and dirty. He was bleeding in five places he could see right away, and he could tell his face was bleeding too.

"This is crazy," he whispered—to himself and to the vines around his wrists and ankles. They loosened, just a little. "Even if that weird old nurse was telling the truth—and I doubt she was—am I about to knock on the door of this crazy house looking like this?"

The vines pulled away from him. The path behind him, back to the street and away from this house, cleared. Brendan took a last look at the house, at the shuttered windows hidden behind ivy and briar. "Besides, what if the nurse was telling the truth? What if the girl in there is really . . ."

Brendan ran from the house, suddenly afraid that someone might be watching him from one of those shuttered, overgrown windows. His book bag bounced heavily on his back as he descended Willow Avenue.

~6~

"I blew it," Brendan said as he slumped into the chair in the nurse's office.

The nurse got one look at him—head to toe covered in scrapes and messy bandages and welts and bruises—and gasped. "Boy, you sure did," she said.

She nodded toward the exam room. "Get in there. I'll clean up these bandages. Who put these on?"

"I did," said Brendan as he hopped up onto the exam table. "Didn't I do a good job?"

He looked down at his arm: the bandages—he'd needed fourteen of them—were wrinkled and loose, hanging off in places and exposing the dried blood and dirty scrapes underneath.

"Do I need to answer that?" the nurse said, and in a flash, with no warning, she tore the dirty bandages from his skin.

"Ow!" Brendan snapped, jerking his arm away. "Let me know next time, okay?"

"Will there be a next time?" she asked, and her eyebrows danced.

"Maybe," he admitted. "I still want to get inside that house. . . . But I don't really know why."

The nurse patted his book bag, which lay beside him on the exam table. "It's the magic," she whispered. "I'd know it anywhere."

Brendan lifted his chin and whispered back,

"I think I could have made it to the door. I was close."

"Yeah?" the nurse said. She swabbed his wounds with alcohol and he winced and sucked his teeth.

"Not that close," Brendan admitted. "It's the vines. I think they're alive."

"Well, yes. Vines usually are," the nurse said. She unwrapped some gauze and wrapped his arm.

"I mean alive like animals, not like regular plants," Brendan explained. "They grabbed me. They didn't want me to go to the house."

"No, I expect they didn't," the nurse said as she taped up the fresh bandage. She stepped back to consider the cuts and scrapes on his cheeks. "Her father is as magic as she is. Get up from there and wash your face. Use the soap next to the sink here."

"Tell me what you mean," Brendan said. He hopped down and went to the sink and turned on the tap. "What exactly is going on up there?"

He pumped the orange soap three times and lathered up his face.

"He was obsessed," the nurse said. "I think he spent a little too much time in his books, but who knows. Careful there. You're splashing everywhere."

"Sorry," said Brendan. He finished rinsing his face and fumbled for the paper towels. The nurse handed him a couple. "Go on."

"The girl was adventurous," the nurse said. "She liked to read, but she also liked to live. She was the type of five-year-old to climb the biggest tree, to explore the darkest and deepest caves, and to plod through the soggiest marshes."

Brendan pictured this girl—dirty and strong, with crooked, short hair the color of wet clay—stomping around the reedy shore of a lake, sliding down a gravel path into the depths of the earth, and running through a dark wood and waving a stick over her head like a sword.

"I remember the day well," the nurse said. She settled into the chair next to the desk and stared at the wall behind Brendan. "She'd been out, as usual, playing in the woods behind the house. They run all the way down the other side of the hill, right to the river and the caves and the marshes. It was heaven for her."

"Sounds nice," Brendan said.

"She was careless," the nurse went on. "She was always so careless. She never cared about what she was doing, or if it was raining, or if the ground was slippery or the rocks were loose. And that day—it wasn't even breakfast yet—it had been raining. It only cleared up for a moment and she was out the door and into the wild.

"She must have slipped," the nurse said, her face pale and faraway. "I can't think how else it could have happened." She stared beyond Brendan, and her eyes shone.

"What happened?" Brendan said.

The nurse seemed to wake up, considering the boy for the first time. With a sigh, she stood up and leaned toward him. She swabbed his cheek and his cuts stung, but this time he didn't flinch.

"The poor thing took a tumble," she said. "She broke her neck, her leg, her arm. The doctor said she was lucky not to be paralyzed. As it is, she can hardly walk—the last time I saw her."

"Is she, like, in a wheelchair?" Brendan said.

The nurse nodded. "Usually," the nurse said. "She was learning crutches when I left. But I doubt she ever uses them."

"Why?"

"Like I said, her father was obsessed with protecting her after that," the nurse said. She pressed a strip of gauze against his cheek and taped it down. "He sealed up the house. Threw out the TVs, the phones, the computers—he even burned all the books. Then he fired the staff—that is, me—and planted briars and vines and thorn bushes. If you ask me, he placed a spell on the place."

Brendan thought she was probably right.

"No one has contact with the outside world," the nurse said, as if to sum up. "Not Mr. Sova or Ms. Sova or little Talia."

Brendan whispered the name back to her: "Talia."

"It's pretty, isn't it?" the nurse said. She shrugged one shoulder. "My idea."

She stood back. "You're all set," she said. "Next time, wear long sleeves and a beekeeper mask or something."

Brendan picked up his book bag.

"They must be half insane by now," the

nurse muttered. "Locked up all these years. She's your age by now, I suppose, and probably a zombie. Might as well have been sleeping for ten years."

* * *

Brendan skipped the rest of the day. He hurried home—no reading, no meandering, no getting lost. At home, he went straight to the garage.

They'd just moved in. His mom hadn't had the chance or the desire to investigate the junk the previous owners had accumulated and deposited to collect rust and dust.

But Brendan had popped his head in once or twice, and he'd spotted something hanging from some nails on the far wall.

He climbed through the rubble and the wreckage, over piles of junk and hidden treasures, and he ignored it all. He kept his eyes on the dull gray blade, high on the plain garage wall.

On his toes, standing on a dry and cracked old tire, he could just reach it. He wrapped his hand around the hilt of the machete and pulled it from the wall.

∿7∿

Brendan marched up Willow Avenue. He found it this time not with magic, but with an online map. Now, with the rusty old machete looped across his back through the straps of his book bag, he climbed Oldtown's highest street.

The Sova House stood at the hill's peak, and the sun was setting behind it, casting it in an orange and pink aura. Beams of white and dusty light shone between the vines.

The iron gate still stood open, and Brendan slipped through and drew his machete. He hacked and he tore and he sliced at the vines. They fought back—he thought they might— grabbing at his wrists and tearing his clothes. But Brendan gritted his teeth. He chopped with all his strength, remembering the fantasy heroes of his thick paperbacks and heavy hardcover tomes.

The vines couldn't fight back fast enough or strong enough. The boy's machete spun and whirled and slashed like a combine, cutting down the overgrowth and clearing the paved path to the front door. When Brendan reached it, he looked back at the open gate, and the path was littered with scraps and twigs and leaves and torn vines.

His brow dripped with sweat, and his shirtsleeves—he'd worn a heavy work shirt today, remembering the cuts of the previous afternoon—were torn right up to his shoulders. The thorny vines had put up a better fight than he thought. Fresh scratches, like random lines of red ink, dashed up and down his arms. His face, too, stung with the perfect little wounds, as precise and narrow as a surgeon's incision.

Brendan took a deep breath and a long look at the Sova House's huge front door. In its day, it would have been a sight: thick, huge, and made of ornate, dark-colored wood. In its center was a diamond-shaped stained-glass window, depicting a child in bed, surrounded by figures. Her parents were easy to pick out, kneeling together beside the bed. There were other people as well, though, and they made Brendan shiver.

They stood together at the foot of the bed, all of them tall and slim and dressed in long, almost translucent robes, and each wore an ornament as a headpiece. One was a star, one was a moon, one was the sun, and one was a skull. Aside from the odd crowns, though, the four looked identical.

Brendan stared at the image, lit from within, until the characters seemed to swim in his vision. They began to move. The parents at the bedside hiccupped with woe. The figures at the foot leaned together, as if they were speaking—consulting.

As Brendan stared, their voices grew from the whisper of wind in the vines all around him to hushed tones, and then to intelligible voices.

"She will die," said the figure who wore a skull. Her voice—it sounded like a woman, but Brendan couldn't be sure—was gravelly and thin. It was like the air rushing out of a closed tomb, opened after thousands of years.

"No," said the others—the sun and the star and the moon. Their voices together rang in a three-part harmony. Together they sounded like crystal, if crystal could talk—or sing. "She will sleep."

The skull nodded slowly and dropped to her knees. The others followed, but they kept their heads high, and the girl on the bed rolled over and pulled up her knees.

Then it was over. It was as if a film had ended and the TV screen went blank. Brendan's face was only inches from the stained-glass window now, and the picture it held was as static and drab as any other. He shook his head, as if that would restore his sanity, and found the doorbell. When he pressed it firmly, it crumbled under his finger.

"Hello!" he shouted through the door. He pounded on the heavy wood, and the sound echoed down the hill, all through Oldtown, but the door stood closed. No footsteps sounded inside.

"Is anyone there?" he called, pounding again. Still there was no response.

Brendan stepped back to get a better look at the house. Aside from the light on in the entryway behind the heavy door, a dim light flickered in a window on the first floor.

Brendan tightened his grip on the machete, and—with a deep breath and returning determination—set his sights on that window.

~ 8 ~

Vines gripped his wrists. They strangled him and tore at him. They ripped his clothes and scratched his face.

He fell once, and the vines came up from the earth and held him. He swung his machete—his sword. Vines split and released him, and others came up to held him down.

With all his strength, he got to his feet, tearing vines and briar at their roots. His shoes were gone—lost in the mud and detritus of the

wild garden. He reached the window, and he peered in, and she was there.

The flickering light came from a lamp—an old one, burning some horrid and smelly gas, so it cast a lurid and sickly light over the girl's face. And the girl: she sat there, hunched and tired, her eyes half closed and her mouth half open. She had a plain face, with a sharp nose, made sharper in the low flickering light. Her hair was short and jagged, like she'd cut it herself, and, though it was tinted green through the window, Brendan could tell it was the color of wet clay.

He knocked on the glass. She didn't flinch. He knocked louder, and she only stared.

"The nurse was right," he muttered. "She's a zombie."

Brendan raised his machete.

9

Smash!

The butt of the machete sent the hundred-year-old pane of glass shattering into the little lamp-lit room. The girl jumped, finally lifted—just the tiniest bit—from her stupor.

Brendan knocked away the shards still in the window frame and climbed inside. He dropped his heavy book bag and knelt beside the girl. She gaped at him, and he smiled up at her. Her eyes, now wide open, were a startling pale blue. The contrast with the deep orange of her hair seemed magical.

"Are you all right?" he asked her, but she didn't reply.

She saw him—he could tell she saw him. But it was like he was barely there, like she was seeing him through a fog or a dream.

"The magic," he whispered, and he opened his book bag and dumped it out on the floor. He grabbed a book at random and held it out to her. She glanced at it, like one might glance at a familiar stranger in a crowd. And Brendan began to read.

He read her the story of an assistant pig keeper, destined to be a hero and king.

He told her of travelers to Mars, and the eerie surprises they found there.

He read to her the love story of a girl and a boy who would live forever.

He didn't know what stories she loved, back when she was allowed to read them, so he chose book after book, and he told her the magic inside.

She smiled just a little at each telling, until finally she was kneeling on the floor with him, pawing through the pile and savoring the stories she found inside.

"You're awake now," Brendan said, and she took his hand in hers and thanked him.

"But you have to go," she said. "You have to go right now."

Brendan stood up and pulled her to her feet. "Why?" he said. "I came to find you. To meet you. The nurse at school—she said we—"

The girl cut him off, shaking her head and urging him backward to the window. "My father," she said. "He'd never allow this. He'll be furious."

But the overhead light flicked on, casting its pallid glare over the dust and dank in the room.

Her face was so pale, so ill, though life began to shine. Brendan pulled his eyes from her face, though, and found the door. There, with his hand still on the light switch and a beard as long as his arms, stood Mr. Sova.

~10~

"I always knew you'd come," Mr. Sova snarled. He dragged Brendan by his tattered collar, and his book bag with the other hand, along the worn and dusty carpet of the house's main hall. With his shoulder, Mr. Sova smashed into the parlor—a huge room with a high ceiling and gigantic fireplace, which swelled with a raging blaze.

"Please," Brendan said, his voice straining and ragged. "I mean no harm!"

"Father," the girl said, grabbing at the man's arm, pleading and tearful. "Let him go. He only wanted to help me!"

"Help you?!" Mr. Sova shouted, his face red and his eyes dark and swollen. "You so quickly trust the intentions of a stranger? One who would smash his way into our home?"

He laughed and shook his head as he dropped the boy into a chair and the book bag in a heap beside the fire. "Sit there, boy," he snarled, "and watch."

He reached down and picked up a book— the biggest one he could find. It was heavy and thick and bound in cloth, tattered at the corners. It was well read and well loved. Mr. Sova read the cover. "Witchcraft," he said in a deep and somber voice. "That's the story here."

He tossed it into the blaze, which coughed and heaved, like a hungry wolf on a too-large bite of deer. Mr. Sova reached for another book. The girl ran at him.

"No, Father!" she demanded. But he merely held her back with one hand and used the free one to grab one, two, three slim paperbacks. He looked at one cover and said, "Rebelliousness," and tossed it into the fireplace.

He looked at the second: "Unrealistic romance," he said, "and suicide." He threw it into the fire.

He looked at the third: "Nonsensical fantasy," he said. That book, too, fell to the hungry tongues of the fire.

He turned to his daughter—down on one knee, tears on her cheeks—and he looked at her with a caring eye. "Talia," he said. "I'll not lose you again—not to this boy, not to the lies in these books, not to the horrors of the world outside our safe walls."

"Safe as houses," said a woman's voice.

Brendan looked up. Standing in the broken parlor doorway was a woman, tall but bent, with long hair—dark at its tips but white at its roots—was braided but falling still to her narrow hips. She looked tired and sad, with the same circles under her eyes that her daughter and husband also wore.

"Isn't that what you said, dear?" Ms. Sova said, for who else could it be? She moved into the room and put a gentle hand on her daughter's shoulders. The girl got to her feet.

"I stand by it," Mr. Sova said. He kicked the pile of books. A slim hardcover fell from the heap. Ms. Sova picked it up.

"Ah," she said, looking at the cover. "This was one of my favorite when I was in school." She moved toward her daughter and held the book out to her. "We read it together, your father and I. Remember that, dear?"

Mr. Sova nodded and smirked.

"Look at her," Ms. Sova said as she took her daughter's face in her hands. "She's so pale and weak. We've nearly destroyed her."

"Nonsense!" Mr. Sova said. "She's alive, isn't she?"

Brendan pulled himself out of the chair, though it hurt every inch of him to do so. He hadn't realized how taxing the evening had been, but the cuts and bruises—not to mention the way Mr. Sova had handled him—had left Brendan feeling utterly beaten.

"Is she?" he said, and his voice was as battered as his body. "She sits like a zombie in front of an ancient box all day, every day, doing what?"

"Learning," Mr. Sova roared. "She's learning important things. Heaven knows what they teach in those schools these days, with these books." He kicked the pile once more.

"Don't you see, dear," said his wife. She faced him now and kept one arm around her daughter's sagging shoulders. "This is what we've been waiting for."

"What?" he said. Then he scoffed and

turned his back on her. "I don't know what you're talking about."

Ms. Sova helped her daughter sit down. Brendan hurried to the girl's side and sat with her.

"You've forgotten," Ms. Sova said. "I have too—from time to time—but this boy has awakened me. You and I have become something unhuman as well, dear. We've been cut off from the world, just as Talia has."

Mr. Sova dropped himself into one of the high-back chairs that flanked the fireplace. He leaned his head on his hand and his elbow on the arm of the chair.

"The spell," Ms. Sova said. She sat on her husband's knee. "This boy is the one we've been waiting for—only we gave up, and we forgot to wait. We forgot to know him."

Mr. Sova looked at his wife and his glare softened. He glanced at Brendan, tattered and beaten, sitting next to his daughter on the settee. "Him?" he said. "Look at him. He barely made it through."

"Dear," said his wife, but he went on.

"Why, a delivery man at the wrong address got as far as the front door not last week," Mr. Sova said.

"That was four years ago, dear," said Ms. Sova.

He coughed. "Was it?" he said, and his eyes darted in his head and his mouth twisted like he was trying to remember the taste of some out-of-season fruit. He stood up in front of Brendan. "But him? I mean, really. Look at him!"

His wife stepped up behind him. She shook her head and said, "Look at her."

Brendan watched a smile come to life on the man's face, behind that Rip Van Winkle beard. It was slow to wake up, just like Talia had been from her stupor in the pallid light of the lamp.

But Brendan could see where the smile was coming from. He turned to Talia beside him on the little dusty couch, and her face glowed. Yes, from the swelling flames of the hearth, but also from her eyes and the apples of her cheeks. She was grinning, with one hand on Brendan's hand between them on the couch and her eyes on the paperback in her other hand. Quietly, while her parents and Brendan clashed, she'd pulled it from the pile and begun to read.

"She's alive again," Ms. Sova said. "Really and truly. She walked on her own. She smiles now, and we have this boy to thank."

Mr. Sova's grin, growing till then, collapsed to a frown.

"I suppose we do," he said. "That's what that old witch said, isn't it? That she'd sleep, stupefied—and we along with her—until love found her. She said until love slashed its way into our home and into her heart."

Ms. Sova leaned on his shoulder and held

his arm. She smiled and gazed at her daughter as Talia tightened her grip on Brendan's hand.

"I'm sorry," said Mr. Sova. He looked at Brendan and said in a firm voice, "What's your name?"

"Shush!" Talia snapped, looking up from her book for an instant. "This is a really good part!"

~11~

That Saturday morning, Brendan was at the Sova House just as the family finished breakfast. Mr. Sova and he, both dressed in heavy denim and long sleeves and thick leather gloves, armed with machetes—gleaming and sharp—and clippers, attacked the wild garden. They hacked it and cut it and shaped it.

At lunchtime, they sat on a bench—it had been lost under the growth all these years—and ate sandwiches and drank iced tea.

"You never told me," Mr. Sova said, "but I think I've guessed."

"Told you what?" Brendan said. He had to squint and shade his eyes when he turned to look at Mr. Sova—the sun behind and above the man was bright and big, as if finally able to attack the Sova House. With its shade hewn and gone, it would now attack without mercy, sweltering and blinding.

The man's face—just yesterday pale and tired, with a beard laughably long—was now clean shaven and red with sunburn. He smiled, the littlest bit, so heavy lines grew on his cheeks. "It was the old nurse, wasn't it?" he said. "She works at the school now, isn't that right?"

"I found your house by accident," Brendan said. "I get lost a lot. But yes. It was the nurse who told me who was inside. I think she must have known . . ." Mr. Sova leaned forward, waiting for Brendan to finish.

"She knew about the spell," Brendan said, "and I think she knew I was the one to end it."

Talia's father leaned back on the bench and looked down Willow Avenue. "I'd say she knew about it," he said. "She placed the spell on our house."

Brendan opened his mouth to speak, but nothing came out. What could he say?

Then he remembered the stained-glass window, and the funny little movie he'd seen— or he thought he'd seen.

He had probably just imagined it, exhausted and bleeding, inhaling magical plant spores all afternoon.

Still . . . it had seemed so real.

"Did she . . ." he started. He faltered and coughed.

"Yes?" Mr. Sova said, leaning forward.

"A crown," Brendan said. "Something like a crown—a wreath."

"That's right," said Mr. Sova.

Brendan stood up, dazed. "Then it was real," he said.

Mr. Sova looked up at him and nodded slowly. He dropped his head. "It was real."

"Then she would have died," Brendan said.

"But we made a deal," Mr. Sova said. He looked past Brendan again, toward Oldtown's village square at the bottom of Willow Avenue, bustling on a sunny autumn Saturday. "She saved our daughter—spared her, really—and we agreed to her terms."

Brendan knelt in front of Mr. Sova. The man seemed to be mourning his daughter all over again, as if she really had died that day, ten years ago.

"Spared her," Brendan said, and then he saw it clearly. "She lied to me."

"Lied?" Mr. Sova said.

"She said Talia fell," Brendan said. "She said

it was an accident. That she broke her neck, and her legs. I never imagined it was her fault."

"Ah," said Mr. Sova, waggling a finger in the air and grinning, "fault is a difficult thing to place, as always."

"Then it was an accident?" Brendan asked.

Suddenly Mr. Sova stood up from the bench and threw back his shoulders. He nodded at the street, at a figure walking there—walking toward them.

"Ask her yourself," said Mr. Sova, "for our old nurse walks this way."

Brendan looked down the hill and spotted that familiar figure—the nurse from school. But she was different today.

This wasn't the same as seeing a teacher at the grocery store or the local pizzeria, when their casual clothes and air made them seem foreign and weird.

This was something quite real.

She stood up straighter and walked with a posture unimaginable in the school's hallways. Her hair—usually tied up in a bun or back in a ponytail—flowed down from her head, no longer gray, but silver, shimmering in the high sun. And her clothes—these were not the typical jeans and sweater of a school faculty member on her day off. Her gown shimmered like her hair, woven with silver and gold thread, and it hung about her like it was made of the icy wind on a February morning.

"What do you want?" Mr. Sova said. Though his words were brave and stubborn, Brendan heard the tremble of fear in his voice.

The nurse must have heard it too, because she laughed out loud. In her voice, Brendan heard the crystal of the sun and the moon and the star, but he also heard the raspy threat of the skull.

"She's all of them," he whispered, almost to himself.

He felt Mr. Sova's hand on his shoulder, just for instant, as if to say that Brendan was right, but also as a warning: *This nurse is dangerous.*

"I only come for my old position," the nurse said, "now that you're all awake."

Mr. Sova let out a sorrowful sigh.

"And Talia?" the nurse said. She sat on the bench and smoothed the lap of her gown. "She is well?"

"Yes," said Talia's father in a deep, reluctant voice.

"Wonderful," said the nurse. She caught Brendan's eye and smiled at him. "Mr. Sova is reluctant to have me back, I think."

Brendan didn't reply. He just stared at her face, and he imagined he could see all four of those figures within her.

She laughed her crystal laugh and patted her hands on her knees. "He remembers how close the girl came to death," she says, still smiling, "but he forgets it was I who pulled her back."

"It was you who sent her there!" Mr. Sova said, and his body quivered and deflated.

She didn't look at him, despite his explosion. She kept her eyes on Brendan. "He sees things in black and white," she said, patting the bench beside her. "He always has."

Brendan sat next to her and sat at an angle to face her. "Who are you?" he asked.

She looked at him, sort of cockeyed, like a confused dog—like it was the most obvious thing in the world, and maybe Brendan had taken a knock on the head. "I'm your nurse," she said. "Don't you remember?"

"But that's not at all you are," Brendan said quickly.

"And you," she said, "are not only the new boy in school."

Brendan thought he knew what she meant.

He still felt dizzy and blinded, though, as the nurse stood up. "I'll go and check on Talia," she said.

"No," Mr. Sova protested, grabbing her wrist.

The nurse looked down at his hand—in that instant, Brendan was sure he saw that skull on her forehead, just like he'd seen her in the stained-glass window—and Mr. Sova released her.

When she spoke, the crystal in her voice was gone, and only the smoky whisper remained: "You cannot hold me back. You cannot control me. You cannot stop me."

Then, with the same grace she carried as she walked up Willow Avenue, the nurse stepped around the bench and walked up the path, opened the door, and went inside the Sova House.

~12~

Though Brendan spent much of his time at the Sova House after that day, and nearly all the rest of his time at school, he didn't see much of the nurse. She resigned from the school, and the new nurse—though competent in every way and very kind to Brendan when he'd show up with a bruised knee and scraped chin, evidence of another run-in with Chunk—she wasn't magical.

At the Sova House, the nurse stayed in her room on the third floor. She appeared now and then, passing through the second-floor hallway or wandering the garden as dusk fell over the house.

In fact, except at those odd moments— when Brendan found he hardly recognized the old school nurse, instead seeing her like a dream, a spirit, a ghost from distant time— Brendan hardly thought about the nurse. He was in love, after all, with Talia, and she with him, and the two spent most of their time reading stories and telling stories to each other.

"We'll get married," Talia told him.

"Of course," Brendan told her.

And that day after school, the two walked with their hands clasped together—and each, with the other hand, held a book to read. Of course they got lost, as they often did, and they would continue to for their rest of their lives together.

~13~

They did get married, Brendan and Talia, and they did stay in the Sova House. The old nurse stayed there too, in her room up on the third floor, and after many years, Brendan and Talia forgot about her.

If someone had asked, "Didn't that nurse used to live up there?" they certainly would have remembered, if only for that instant. But they never thought of her, and when they glimpsed her only briefly, floating down a hall or through the manicured gardens, they only rubbed their eyes and poured a second cup of coffee.

They had three daughters, and they were named Roxanne, Dawn, and Aurora, the youngest. Only Aurora, perhaps due to her youth, truly saw the old nurse. She watched her closely and caught her smiles and her glares, and she tried to touch the hem of her shimmering gown. She never quite could, though.

Aurora also spent a lot of time in the kitchen. Her parents were quite successful, and as is often the case with great success, they were also quite busy. Neither had much time— nor the desire—to cook, so they hired a cook.

"Brendan loves lamb," Talia said with a pad on one knee.

"I make a wonderful lamb," the cook said. She was heavy and dour, and her plump face was freckled and blotchy—whether from sun or allergies or nerves, no one could guess.

"And the girls will insist on goose," Talia went on.

"I make a beautiful goose," the cook said. She smiled with pride and closed her eyes. With a hum, she seemed to be imagining the flavors of her goose. "Beautiful."

Talia went on. "And I," she said, "could not go on if our cook didn't have a marvelous recipe for pork loin."

"Then you're in luck," the cook whispered. "Mine is the most marvelous you'll ever try."

Talia smiled and closed her pad. "You can begin at once?" she asked, and the cook nodded, and so she took the job.

Aurora and the cook became fast friends. The littlest Miren girl climbed the tallest kitchen stool and sat at the counter, watching dough and sauce and cake and scones come together. "How many eggs?" she asked, or

"How much flour?" or "Do you need the baking soda?" So it was the cook, rather than her mother or father or sisters, whom Aurora first talked to about the wandering spirit of the nurse on the third floor.

The cook spat. "Haunted," she said, and she looked around the huge old kitchen as though it had been keeping something from her. "I shouldn't be surprised."

"I think it's a kind ghost," the little girl said, and she shifted on the stool to reach the biggest wooden spoon. "At least, it usually is. Sometimes it hisses at me."

"Hm," said the cook. She measured out two cups of flour, and then one-third of a cup. She dumped the flour into the largest copper bowl and added a pinch of salt and a tiny spoon of soda and put it in front of the girl. "Stir."

"But usually she smiles," Aurora said, and she held the big spoon with both hands and messily stirred the bowl of dry ingredients.

She flashed the cook a big, toothy grin as she worked.

The cook grunted and cracked an egg, then another, then another, into a second bowl. "I don't like it," she muttered, pulling a whisk from its hook. She began to beat the eggs, her arm thrashing so fast it grew blurry, and her face going puffier and redder. Aurora's stirring slowed as she watched the cook work.

"You should stay away from that spirit," the cook grunted, short of breath. She tossed the whisk into the sink and went to the refrigerator. When she came back with a quart of milk, the girl was gone from the stool and the kitchen. A trail of flour footprints led to the door.

"You should really stay away," the cook muttered as she measured out a cup of milk.

~14~

The Sova House wasn't built in one go. It was the oldest house in Oldtown, built by the first Sovas to settle at the top of that hill. Over the years and decades and generations, rooms had been added and expanded. Walls had been taken down and put back up. Doors had been covered and revealed.

Though her mother had slept through the years she should have been exploring the house, Aurora had no such curse. When it rained—and sometimes when it didn't—she took to finding old passages and hidden doors and rickety back stairways.

It was one day, an especially rainy and thundering summer afternoon, that Aurora lost track of time and steps. She climbed a spiraling staircase behind a little door in the closet in Dawn's bedroom and found herself in a tiny, dark space. Only a sliver of light found its way inside, through a tiny crack near the floor.

Aurora was not the sort of girl to panic. She felt around the sliver of light and traced the outline of a tiny door—no bigger than a volume from her father's set of encyclopedias. There was no handle, though, and no doorknob. When she pushed it, she could tell it was blocked on the outside.

"It's probably a tremendous dresser," she whispered to the darkness, "or the back of a couch."

Aurora decided that the little door would prove a dead end. She was about to head back down the narrow spiral staircase when she heard a great screech on the other side of the door. The floor beneath her began to shake and vibrate. She held on to the railing at the top of the steps, closed her eyes tightly, and shrieked.

"Oh, stop that noise at once," said a voice, and Aurora knew it at once, though she'd never heard it before.

The girl opened her eyes and found that the door was gone. In its place was a square of flickering light and a pair of bare feet caked with soil, with toenails painted silver and gold and glittering, watery green. The feet moved to the side and Aurora crawled and slithered through the tiny door. She barely fit.

"Before long, you'll be far too big for that way in," the spirit said as it walked across the room to the door. This was of course the nurse's chamber on the third floor, and

Aurora's tiny room at the top of the spiral staircase was indeed hidden behind a settee. "Next time, use the door."

The nurse glowered at the girl as Aurora kept her eyes on the floor and walked quickly across the room. The door opened as Aurora reached and she stepped out onto the landing at the top of the central staircase. She faced the nurse. "I'm sorry," she said.

"For what, dear child?" the nurse said, smiling. Her voice was made of ringing bells and shattering glass and feet scraping across gravel.

Aurora stared at the nurse's face, and she couldn't be sure if she was seeing a woman, or a spirit, or several of each.

Thunder boomed outside, and—Aurora counted—three seconds later, the room flashed brightly. "I didn't mean to bother you," the girl said. "I didn't know where that funny staircase would go."

"They always go up," the nurse said, "or down."

"Yes, ma'am," Aurora said. Still she stood in the open doorway and stared at the spirit's face.

"Was there something else, sunshine?" the nurse said.

"The cook thinks I should stay away from you," Aurora said.

"Does she?" the nurse said, and Aurora nodded. "Well, lots of people—especially grown-ups—are afraid of things they can't control."

"Like you?" Aurora said.

"Like me," the nurse said.

Aurora pulled her eyes from the spirit's face, with its shining eyes and gentle smile, and looked at the worn, wood floor.

"You may speak your mind," the nurse said. All roughness vanished from her voice, and Aurora hurried to speak.

"Who are you?" she said.

The nurse laughed, and it was like a concert of bells. Aurora laughed too.

"So few have asked me so directly," she said. "Your father did."

Aurora was stunned. Her father was a middle-aged man. He was more obsessed with his books and his business than with things like spirits and questions. He had ever spoken to this striking figure?

"He was a boy then, of course," the nurse said. "I'll tell you most of what I told him: I am the sum of my parts."

Aurora didn't know what that meant, but she didn't feel confident any longer. She coughed into her fist. "I'll go downstairs now," she said.

"One more thing, sunshine," the nurse said as she retreated to the settee and sat down. "I'm quite hungry. It's been ages since I ate."

"I'll ask Cook to make you something," the girl said. She was excited for an excuse to run to the kitchen and tell the cook everything.

"Would you?" the nurse said. "Wonderful. It will give you a clearer idea of who I am." The nurse picked a book up from the side table and opened it to its middle. "If you please, sunshine, tell your cook that I'd like to have Roxanne for lunch."

"Roxanne?" Aurora repeated. "My sister?"

The nurse nodded, still smiling. Her eyes were black and shone like a polished stone. "With a sauce of butter and mustard."

Aurora stood there, staring from the landing, until the door closed.

~15~

Aurora walked in a daze down two flights of stairs on the wide central staircase. She pushed the swinging door into the kitchen and found Cook, bent over and pulling a sheet of scones from the oven.

"You're just in time, littlest," the cook said as she dropped the sheet onto the center island with a clatter and clank. "We can have one each with cream in a few minutes." She looked at

Aurora and smiled, her brown teeth and ruddy cheeks flaming.

"I've been upstairs," Aurora said, and she didn't smile, and she did not seem to notice the tray of cranberry and orange-zest scones on the island—her favorite flavor. "With the spirit."

The cook gasped, and she clucked her tongue and shook her head. "It can't end well," she said.

"She's hungry," Aurora said, "and you're the cook."

"Not for her," the cook spat. She pulled the second sheet of scones and dropped them onto the cooktop. The triangles—speckled with red and orange—bounced and slid. One fell to the floor, and the cook did not care. "She can have that one," she muttered.

"She lives in this house," Aurora said, "so you have to cook for her."

The cook snorted and went to the

refrigerator. She came back with a tub of cream and dropped it on the island next to the cooling scones.

"She wants Roxanne for lunch," Aurora said.

The cook slammed her open hand on the island, sending another scone to the dirty kitchen floor. She stomped on the fallen scone and coughed with anger. "How can you say this to me?" she said to the girl. The cook's face grew redder and redder—nearly crimson. "Your own sister!"

But Aurora hardly heard the cook. "With a butter and mustard sauce," she finished.

The cook leaned heavily on one hand and tapped her chin with the other. "Go to the refrigerator, littlest," the cook said, "and fetch a goose."

"Didn't you hear me?" Aurora said. "She doesn't want goose."

"Do as I say," the cook said, "and when

you've done that, run and find Roxanne and bring her here as well."

* * *

The cook worked for an hour on the spirit's lunch. The sauce was rich and spicy, and the meat was tender and flavorful. She arranged the choicest cuts on a silver platter, with a pitcher of sauce and a dish of root vegetables and glazed carrots. She covered the platter and gave it to Aurora.

"Bring this up to the fiend," she told her, "and don't join her for lunch. Come back at once."

Aurora did as she was told, but she cried and cried as she walked, for she believed she carried her oldest sister.

When she reached the nurse's door, it stood open. In the center of the room there was now

a small table, set for two. The spirit sat at one seat.

"Hello, sunshine," the nurse said. "Put it here, please." She motioned to the center of the table, and Aurora obeyed. She pulled the cover off to present the dinner.

"Ahh," said the spirit, clapping like a pleased child. She inhaled deeply with her eyes closed, savoring the food's scent.

Aurora was sickened, watching the woman so excited to devour the meal.

"Join me," the spirit said, but Aurora shook her head and hurried out of the room.

~16~

"You'll have to go collect the dishes," the cook said when Aurora returned, out of breath and crying.

"I don't want to," Aurora said.

"I can't climb all those steps," the cook said. She collapsed into her chair near the window and took a deep breath of the air from her herb garden outside. "You're young and healthy and you'll collect the dishes."

Aurora stamped her foot, but she knew the cook was right. But rather than hurry up to the spirit's room, she went to Dawn's room. Dawn lay on her bed on her belly with a book open on the pillow.

"What do you want?" said the middle sister, looking up from her paperback. Aurora recognized it at once as one of Dad's old fantasy stories.

"Nothing," Aurora said. She sat down on the edge of the bed next to her sister. "I just wanted to say hi."

"Hi," Dawn said. "Now get out so I can finish reading."

Aurora got up from the bed, took a last look at Dawn, and slipped into the closet. Her sister, engrossed in the fantasy story, didn't even notice.

Up the twirling staircase in the dark. Aurora thought about the shape of the stairs and the darkness in the stairwell and the musty smell and the age of the house. At the top she crawled to the crack of light near the floor and she listened.

She heard the spirit, chewing and slurping, loudly devouring. She heard the snapping of brittle, cooked bones. She smelled the spice of the mustard in the sauce, and the sickly sweet of the sugared carrots. Aurora pounded on the tiny door as she cried.

"You'll use the door," the spirit said after she'd pushed aside the settee again and let the girl into the room. "Next time, you'll use the door."

Aurora didn't reply. She didn't even look at her. She hurried to the table and, with her eyes closed tight, covered the platter and hurried from the room.

"I'll have dinner now," the spirit called after her, her voice as sparkling as ever. "Bring me Dawn."

Aurora hiccupped and coughed and nearly

dropped the dishes, but she bit her bottom lip and tensed her shoulders. She could not let the spirit see her cry.

"Fetch a lamb," the cook said. "There's one in the freezer. Put it in the sink."

Aurora obeyed, and knew well enough to turn on the cold tap as well to help the goose defrost. She stood at the sink, watching the slim stream of cold water run over the lamb in its vacuum-sealed plastic wrapping. "She said she wants Dawn for supper," Aurora said.

"Do as you're told," the cook snarled, banging roasting pans and metal spoons and sauce pots. "Now go and collect your sister and bring her here."

Aurora left the tap running, climbed down from her stool, and plodded across the kitchen and through the swinging door.

She stopped for a moment at the window seat near the front door and looked out into the garden. The spirit was there, walking across the muddy ground, even though it was raining hard.

Thunder clapped while Aurora watched, and she counted: one, two—and the sky lit up white. The instant it did, the spirit flicked her eyes onto the girl and grinned, and Aurora gasped.

★ ★ ★

"Come to the kitchen," Aurora said, standing in Dawn's open doorway.

"Why?" said her sister without looking up from her book.

Aurora sniffled and shook her head.

"Ugh," Dawn said. She folded down the corner of her page and got up from the bed. "Fine."

Aurora led her sister down the main stairs and through the swinging door.

"It stinks in here," Dawn said. "What are you cooking?"

The cook's knife slammed onto the cutting board, crushing a head of garlic to a sticky and smelly paste.

~17~

"I have your supper," Aurora said. Trails of tears stained her cheeks, but she didn't cry as she stood in the open doorway of the spirit's room. The rain on the roof sounded like gentle applause.

"Finally," the ghostly woman said as she took a seat at the small table. "You'll join me this time."

Aurora put the platter in the center of the

table. She pulled off the lid, and the steam wafted up at her and stung her eyes till they ran.

"Wonderful!" the spirit said, her shining eyes wide with gluttony. For an instant, her smile fell and her eyes darkened, and she looked at Aurora. "We will devour her."

But Aurora didn't take her seat and she didn't reply. She merely hurried from the room, down the stairs, past Dawn's bedroom—where the door stood open and the light was still on—and to the kitchen.

"Is she satisfied?" the cook said, but Aurora ran at her and collapsed into her open arms. The cook held her in a hug as strong as the Sova House, and she ran a meaty hand over her hair to soothe her. "There, littlest. There, there. You'll collect the dishes before too long."

★ ★ ★

The spirit lay on the settee on her back, one hand in the air as if conducting an invisible orchestra. She stared at the ceiling. "The rain is like a song," she said, and her voice was soft and oily.

Aurora stood beside the little table. The platter was clean, with only smears of the butter and mustard sauce left. Every vegetable and every speck of meat was gone.

"You missed a wonderful meal," the spirit said, still conducting the rain.

Aurora piled the plates and forks and knife on the platter and covered it. She hefted it and left the room.

"I'm not satisfied," the spirit called after her. "I'll need a little something before bedtime."

Aurora stopped.

"Just the littlest something," the spirit said, and Aurora dropped the platter. It clattered down the main stairs, plates shattering and the large silver dome lid ringing like an alarm bell.

★ ★ ★

The cook found the girl on the second-floor landing, lying on her side and clutching her belly. "She's still hungry," Aurora said, but her voice was rough and raw from crying.

The cook gathered her up and carried her downstairs, through the swinging door, and into the kitchen. She sat her on her stool at the counter.

"There's a pork loin in the basement deep freeze," the cook said. "I'll go and fetch it. You stay right there."

"But she doesn't want pork," Aurora stuttered through the hiccups of her sobbing.

"Do as you're told," the cook growled, and she disappeared down the rickety basement steps.

Aurora sat on her stool, and soon she

stopped crying, and then she stopped sniffling, and then she stopped hiccupping. Then she heard whispering and hisses from the big pantry with the heavy wooden door.

The littlest Miren climbed down from her stool and went to the pantry. The handle—heavy and metal and tightly latched—was always tricky for her, so she put both hands on the thing and tugged with all her might and weight.

The latch popped, and the heavy door began to swing open.

"Who is it?" came a fearful whisper from within.

"It's that lousy cook," came a second whisper, "who locked us in here to rot."

"Like this head of lettuce," said the first, and then the whispers giggled.

"Roxanne?" Aurora said, peering into the dark pantry. "Dawn?"

"Let us out of here!" Dawn said, running for the door, but the cook's heavy hands fell on to Aurora's shoulders.

"And littlest makes three," the cook snarled. Aurora fell forward, knocking the middle sister back and into the darkness. Then the door slammed closed and the latch clicked.

~18~

"Aw, nuts," said Dawn. In the dark pantry, Aurora couldn't see her sisters, but she heard the middle girl kick something—probably one of cook's giant flour sacks. "Nice going, runt."

"Don't blame her," Roxanne said. Her voice was always so still and rich; it reminded Aurora of cold gravy. "She didn't know the cook was behind her."

"Yeah, yeah," said Dawn. She kicked the sack of flour again. Aurora could smell the dust of it in the heavy pantry air.

"Are you ghosts?" Aurora said quietly, as if the pantry was the church and her sisters its spirits.

"What is she talking about?" Dawn said.

"Beats me," Roxanne said. Aurora felt the air shift as her oldest sister moved toward her. "You all right, sunshine?"

Aurora shivered at the nickname. Though it was hers often enough among the three of them, lately she only heard it from the nurse in the attic. Aurora realized she was crying, and, shaking her head, she reached blindly for Roxanne's hand. She found her arm and pulled it around her.

"Whoa, what happened?" Dawn said, joining her sisters by the giant can of olives near the door.

Dawn always started out so cold, but when she warmed up, she became loving and lovable, and that made Aurora sob even more. Her poor older sisters, still clueless about why they'd been locked in the pantry, had to wait and soothe her and coo in her ear until she was calm and collected enough to tell them everything.

But finally she did, and then the two older sisters cried too: they cried because they were afraid and relieved to be alive and so thankful for the cook and how she'd saved them.

"But won't we have to stay in here forever?" Roxanne said.

Aurora had to admit she didn't know. She hadn't been part of the cook's plan, and she couldn't guess what the spirit would do when she found out the girls still lived.

As she sat there, wrapped in her sisters' arms and love, she thought it over. Would the cook be able to climb the two flights to the spirit's room to deliver the pork loin that was meant to be Aurora?

Then there came a great crash from the other side of the pantry door.

"What trickery is this!" shrieked the spirit. The crystal in her voice shattered.

"Get back," the cook roared at the spirit. "You're not welcome in here."

The spirit laughed—the sound now was so chilling that Aurora shook in Roxanne's arms. "This house belongs more to me than to you, cook," the spirit said. "It belongs more to me than to the Sovas themselves."

"Lies," said the cook. "You are a wicked thing and every word you utter is a lie." She spat. "Out."

"I hear them whispering," the nurse said. "What did you feed me?" The cook didn't answer, but an instant later there was a great clatter and the rattle of pans being thrown and big metal spoons falling in piles to the tile floor.

The girls heard the cook grunting and howling in pain. Then everything was quiet.

"She's coming for us," Aurora whispered, and her sisters nodded. "We have to get out of here."

"How, runt?" Dawn said. "The door is locked from the outside."

"Come with me," Aurora said. "Hold my hand so we don't get lost." And she led her sisters deeper into the huge pantry, all the way to the back corner. There, she needed Roxanne's help to heave bags of flour out of the way, and then a big can of tomato paste, and then a wooden crate lid leaning against the wall. It revealed a sliver of light, right in the corner.

"What is it?" Dawn said.

"It's a secret," Aurora said. "This house has a lot of secrets."

"Boy, I'll say," Dawn muttered.

Aurora crouched down on her knees at the sliver of light and felt around with her fingers. She found a tiny latch.

The nurse's gentle footsteps echoed on the other side of the pantry door.

"She's coming," Roxanne whispered.

Aurora twisted the tiny latch.

The pantry door clicked and began to open.

Aurora stood up and kicked at the sliver of light, and the secret little door sprung open. "Hurry," Aurora said, and the three girls dropped to the floor and slithered out and closed the door behind them.

"Where are you?" the spirit sang in the pantry behind them. They heard cans and jars and boxes crash to the hard pantry floor as the nurse searched for them.

"Now what?" Roxanne hissed. "She'll figure out we're not there pretty quick."

But Aurora had thought of that, and she

was already planning. The tiny door had let the girls out in the guest bathroom, right next to the sink. Aurora got up from the chilly tile floor and ran from the room. She heard her sisters behind her.

"What are you doing?" Dawn called after her, but Aurora didn't want to take the time to explain. She ran down the main hall, across the foyer, and slammed into the kitchen.

"She'll hear you!" Roxanne said.

Aurora didn't care. She was counting on speed, and she raced across the kitchen floor, only hardly noticing the cook, sprawled out on the tile, groaning in pain. She was pleased that the big woman was alive, and Aurora was smiling as she ran at top speed into the pantry door. It slammed closed with a satisfying thwack. The latch clicked, locking the door.

"Let me out!" the nurse shouted, banging on the door with her fists. "Let me out this instant!"

The cook sat up, shaking her head to clear the knocks and bruises she'd suffered. Aurora put an arm around her big shoulders.

"I'm glad you're okay," she said.

The cook, gulping back tears, took the littlest Miren in her arms. "And I'm glad you are," she said.

The older girls stood nearby, shuffling their feet. They felt awkward, shy, and confused.

"And you two, too," the cook said, "even if you don't think much of me."

"We do," Roxanne said, and she elbowed the middle girl.

"Yes," Dawn said, rubbing her side. "We do."

~19~

When Brendan Miren returned that night to the Sova House after an exhausting day of making books, his daughter Aurora ran to him right away.

"Why aren't you in bed?" he said. "Isn't your mother home yet?"

She wasn't, and Aurora apologized for still being up. She took her father into the main floor guest bathroom. She showed him the

long crack that ran up the wall near the floor next to the sink.

"Hm," he said, rubbing his chin. "I'd better seal that up." And he did, with tape and spackle and plaster. Then Aurora showed him some other cracks in some other walls, and with boards and nails and plaster, he sealed those as well.

The cook stopped using the pantry for storage, and she had to buy quite a lot of flour in the next couple of weeks, not to mention one goose, one pig, and one lamb. But Mr. and Mrs. Miren didn't mind much, and no one noticed that the wandering figure—with soil on her feet and dressed head to toe in shimmering gowns—never appeared in their halls or garden again.

Sleeping Beauty

• ★ • ★ •

Sleeping Beauty is an old fairy tale that's been retold by both the German Brothers Grimm and the famous French author Charles Perrault. It was first published in 1697, but folklorists think it may have existed much earlier than that.

In the traditional story, a baby girl is born in a kingdom. Fairies are invited to become her godmothers and bestow gifts upon her. But one fairy curses the baby girl, saying that she will prick her hand on a spindle and die. Another fairy tries to save the girl, changing the curse to one hundred years of sleep.

Though her family tries to rid the kingdom of spindles, the princess finds one, pricks her finger, and falls asleep. The fairies put everyone in the castle to sleep as well.

One hundred years later, a prince from another kingdom learns of the sleeping people inside the castle. He makes his way through the thorns and to the princess's side. She awakens, and they fall in love.

The prince and princess marry and have children, a boy and a girl. But the prince's stepmother is an ogre, and while the prince is away, she tells her cook to kill and cook the boy. The cook refuses and tricks her with a lamb. Then she tricks her again, this time serving a goat she says is the prince and princess's daughter. When the stepmother finds out the truth, she tries to kill everyone by throwing them into a pit of vipers.

Luckily, the children's father returns and saves his family. The evil stepmother throws herself into the pit of vipers.

Tell your own twicetold tale!

• ★ • ★ •

Choose one from each group, and write a story that combines all of the elements you've chosen.

A boy who finds out he's a prince

A girl who hasn't ever been able to fall asleep

Two sisters who have never met

A young man who angers his father

A stone cottage

A mall

A tall building

A hut

A dog that can
speak

A cat

A sheep

A dolphin

Antarctica

The Amazon River

Ancient Egypt

Texas

An old king

A witch

A man wearing a mask

A little girl with wings

An old, broken mirror

A watch

A photo of a grandmother

A penny

More Twicetold Tales

about the author

Olivia Snowe lives between the falls, the forest, and the creek in Minneapolis, Minnesota.

about the illustrator

Michelle Lamoreaux was born and raised in Utah. She studied at Southern Utah University and graduated with a BFA in illustration. She likes working with both digital and traditional media. She currently lives and works in Cedar City, Utah.